Lizard Walinsky

by ROBERTA BAKER   Illustrated by DEBBIE TILLEY

LITTLE, BROWN AND COMPANY

New York ❧ An AOL Time Warner Company

WGATAP

For Isabel, the real Lizard. I will always love you bigger than space.
And for Jim, with thanks and love.

— R.B.

For Gillian

—D.T.

Text copyright © 2004 by Roberta Baker
Illustrations copyright © 2004 by Debbie Tilley

First Edition

Library of Congress Cataloging-in-Publication Data
Baker, Roberta.
    Lizard Walinsky / by Roberta Baker ; illustrated by Debbie Tilley. — 1st ed.
        p. cm.
    Summary: Lizard, a girl who only likes dinosaurs, and Spider, a boy who loves dinosaurs, spiders, and other creepy things, have a great time together until first grade begins and they are sent to different schools.
    ISBN 0-316-07331-8
    [1. Best friends — Fiction. 2. Friendship — Fiction. 3. Individuality — Fiction. 4. Schools — Fiction.] I. Tilley, Debbie, ill. II. Title.

PZ7. B17485 Li 2003
[E] — dc21   2002028298

10 9 8 7 6 5 4 3 2 1

Book design by Sheila Smallwood

SC

Manufactured in China

The illustrations for this book were done in watercolor and ink.
The text was set in Berling and Providence Sans, and the title type was hand-lettered by Holly Dickens.

Lizard Walinsky would not play mermaids.
She would not wear dresses on special occasions.
And she did not like dolls—especially ones that
wet, talked, or walked.

"I'm a dinosaur girl!" Lizard roared. "Why did
Grandma give me *another* doll?"

The Suzy dolls, Darcy dolls, and Prudence dolls sprouted cobwebs under Lizard's porch.
Their petticoats, tutus, and jumpers stayed buried under Lizard's laundry.
Unless, of course, Lizard put on a dinosaur fashion show.

Want to see what T. Rex wears when he eats Camarasaurus?

"What a lovely nest!" cooed Lizard's mom when she found the Maiasaura guarding socks in Lizard's drawer.

"Your whole room is prehistoric!" cawed Lizard's sister, Lulu. "Don't you play with anything else?"

Every Friday Lizard got three dollars for setting the table, folding the laundry, and cleaning her room.
"Dinosaurs probably became extinct because they had too many chores," she grumbled.
But she did them without complaining too loudly. She was saving to buy the Nanotyrannus at the Hands-On Science Store.

"Want to see my Nanotyrannus swallow a Komodo dragon?" Lizard asked at the playground.

"Not right now," sighed Melody.

"Dinosaurs are extinct," Cassandra snorted. "I'VE moved on to OTHER things."

"It's not that I don't like dinosaurs," Todd said, shrugging. "It's just that I like skateboarding better."

Lizard felt sad and alone.

"Fossil," she said to the family's bulldog, "you're the only dinosaur lover I know."

"If only Elizabeth Ann could find *someone* who shares her interests," Lizard's parents fretted.

That summer, Lizard's dad drove her to T-ball practice. That's where Lizard met Spider.

Spider's real name was Simon. The other kids booed when Spider missed. They screamed when Spider walked near them.

"GET THAT THING AWAY FROM ME!"

Scurrying over sand in Spider's palm was a reddish brown spider the size of a raisin.

"She's beautiful," Lizard whispered.

"Her name's Nectarine," said Spider.

Lizard smiled and thought for a minute. "You wouldn't happen to like dinosaurs, would you?"

"I LOVE dinosaurs!" Spider grinned back.

Lizard and Spider became best friends. They built a terrarium in Spider's basement, complete with cliffs, floodplains, waterfalls, and ferns from the lot next door. Nectarine frolicked among the dinosaur models.

During T-ball, they combed the outfield, rescuing Pteranodon eggs.

At night, they toasted marshmallows and gummy worms and squashed them between peanut-butter cookies.

"We're best friends! We'll never become extinct!" Lizard and Spider cheered.

At the end of summer, Spider gave Lizard his favorite key chain.
Lizard gave Spider her 3-D glasses.
"Let's stay friends until the second Ice Age," she piped. "See you in first grade!"

On the first day of school, Lizard stuffed a dinosaur in each pocket, and one in her snack bag for Spider.

She clutched a fistful of pencils, and a box of creepy creature cards to stump Spider.

But Spider wasn't on the school bus.

He wasn't in Mr. Argyle's class.

He wasn't on the playground at recess.

Spider, raise your hand so I can see you!

Lizard walked home alone from the bus stop.

"Sweetheart, Spider goes to first grade at a different school! You can play with Spider on weekends," said Lizard's mom.

Lizard's heart split like the sides of a volcano.

"I'll never see Spider again...I just know it!" She cried hot lava tears.

At supper, Lizard couldn't eat, even though her mother made quadruple cheese pizza.
"So, how was my big girl's first day?" her father asked.
"I'm not going to first grade," announced Lizard. "I can already count to seventy-three."

The next morning, Lizard's mom drove Lizard to school.
Lizard drooped at the classroom door.
Lizard's mom squeezed Lizard's hand. "When I started first grade,
I had dinosaurs in my tummy, too."

One of the girls made a face when she saw Lizard's
Nanotyrannus. "YUCK! What's that? A big salamander?"
"It's a dinosaur," said Lizard. "If you're not nice to me,
he might eat your snack for lunch."

At recess, while Mr. Argyle's class played hopscotch, jump rope, and hide-and-seek, Lizard built a fort out of blocks. *This is the best fort I ever made*, thought Lizard. *I wish Spider could see it.*

"I like your fort," said Samantha, a girl in Lizard's class. "Can I come in?"

"Maybe tomorrow," Lizard brooded. "Right now I'm a Gigantosaurus who hunts alone."

After school Lizard's mom fixed dinosaur nuggets. Then she said, "I have a special surprise."

On the way to Lizard's favorite playground, they stopped at Spider's house. "GUESS WHAT, LIZARD? Mom says I can get a pet garter snake! If it has babies, I'll give one to you!"

They pretended to be pythons and rattlesnakes.

Lizard hissed. Spider lunged.

"There is only one Lizard Walinsky!" Spider gave Lizard a new secret handshake.

Lizard beamed.

"There is only one Spider, too."

The next day Lizard didn't feel sad about going to school.
For show-and-tell she brought the terrarium she had built with Spider.
"I made this with my best friend," Lizard explained. "It has a waterfall and a hot tub with a slide."

"How boring." Wallace rolled his eyes. "My UFO lights up and spins."
"How silly," Victoria chimed. "My Prudence doll can sing."
"What a cool tank!" Samantha whistled. "Can my salamander try the slide?"

Samantha and Lizard watched the salamander skitter.
Lizard thought for a moment. "You know, your salamander can
live in the terrarium, if you want. Spider wouldn't mind."

TUB-O
BUTTER

Samantha and Lizard sat together for stories. They traded juice boxes at snacktime.
On Saturday, Spider came over to play. Lizard also invited Samantha.
"Samantha?" Spider crinkled his nose. "Don't you have an animal name?"
"You can call me Salamander if you want."

Together they dug a make-believe tar pit and made their own special mud.

Spider sifted. Salamander stirred. Lizard poured.

"Just think," Lizard whispered. "In a hundred million years, we'll have fossils!"

Salamander gulped. "Do we really have to wait that long?"